For My friend
Storm
AKA a "Mr Beens"—
one who leads people
to new normal/new
different

Lovingly
Sue Beeney

10/2011

A JOURNEY WITH
Mrs. Beens

people helping people

NEW HOPE
Grief Support Community

Copyright ©2011
New Hope Grief Support Community
www.newhopegrief.org

Written by Marsha Ann Dobler
Concept by Susan K. Beeney
Illustrations by Julie Kocher and Allison Oh
Type Design by Xiomara Hartzler
Copy Editing by David Barnes
Production Assistance by Alison Barnes
Art Direction by Kurt Simonson
Printed by bigger dot (www.biggerdot.com)
Printed in Korea

ISBN 978-1-4507-1385-6

How to Use This Book Effectively:

• This book is to be used by parents, family members, professional counselors, teachers, medical and care-giving professionals, and others involved in the life of any child 3-9 years old who has suffered the death of a special person.

• This book may be used effectively one-on-one or in a group setting.

• It is recommended that the reader become familiar with this book before reading it to a child. Think about ways to customize the story to fit the grieving child's particular situation. Use age appropriate language that the little one will understand when discussing the story.

• The story was not created to be used in only one session or one setting. Shorter reading sessions will better accommodate a young child's age, brief attention span, and fragile emotional condition during their time of grief.

• Play acting this story might encourage further opportunities for younger children to express their grief.

For more information on supporting a grieving child, please see the back of the book.

A Journey with Mrs. Beens

A CHILDREN'S STORYBOOK OF GRIEF SUPPORT

Written by Marsha Ann Dobler
Concept by Susan K. Beeney

Illustrated by
Julie Kocher and Allison Oh

ONCE upon a time there lived a young Princess Jessica and her brother, Prince Michael. They lived in the castle with their parents, the King and the Queen. They were all very happy together. Their mother, the Queen, would read them stories and take them for long walks in the forest. They would play games together and when they fell and hurt themselves, their mother would bandage their hurts and give them hugs and kisses.

ONE day, the Queen knew that she was very sick. She wanted to do something special for her children. She gave Jessica and Michael two precious gifts. To Jessica, she gave a golden locket. Inside the locket were pictures of the King and the Queen. Jessica loved the locket and promised her mother that she would wear it every day.

The Queen gave Michael a golden pocket watch that had belonged to his favorite grandfather. Michael promised to take care of the watch and keep it safe in his pocket.

ONE day, their daddy the King went to the Queen's bedroom to wake her up. She was very sick. He was worried and called the royal doctor. The doctor said that the Queen had a terrible sickness that would cause her to die very soon. The King loved the Queen so much that he wept loudly and called the children to come to see their mother.

The children cried and clung to their mother as she lay in her bed. She was so ill that she could not speak. Later that day, she died. The children hugged their father and they all cried together. They all felt so lost without their mother. What were they going to do without her?

That night Jessica and Michael cried themselves
to sleep with their father by their sides. Their sadness
was so deep that nothing could make them feel better.
Their lives would never be the same again.

THE next morning, a visitor came to the castle. Her name was Mrs. Beens. The King had sent for her because he knew that she could help them. She smiled at Michael and Jessica and they knew that she understood their sadness. She listened to them as they told her that their dear mother had died and that they were very, very sad. They trusted her.

Mrs. Beens told them that she had come to take them on a journey which would be a long walk. The journey would be very hard for them. But it would help them heal from their deep sadness and at the end of the walk they would feel better. She hugged them both with gentle arms that were like the wings of a dove protecting her young.

MRS. BEENS led the children out of the doors of the castle and through the forest where they had played with their mother. They began their journey.

As they entered the Land of Grief, a place of deep sadness, it became very foggy. They could barely see one another or where they were going. "Mrs. Beens, what is this place?" they asked.

"THIS is Reality Mountain," she explained. "While you climb up the mountain, you will have many strange feelings about your mother and her death. You may feel very confused. The Fog of Strange Feelings makes it hard to know what to do or where to turn, but I will be with you." "Why is it called Reality Mountain?" asked Michael. Mrs. Beens told him that during this part of the journey, it would be hard to believe that his mother had really died. Michael said that he sometimes pretended that his mother was still alive. "You will need to know that this is not pretend, that your mother has truly died. But you will be alright," said Mrs. Beens.

AFTER many days in the fog and climbing up Reality Mountain, the children came upon a dark swamp. Jessica had a horrible feeling about this place. "What is this?" she asked. "These are the Swamps of Sadness, my dear," said Mrs. Beens. "As you go through this part of your journey, you will feel very, very sad because now you really do believe that your mother has died." "Will you hold my hand?" "Of course," said Mrs. Beens. "That is why I am here."

Mrs. Beens said that as they traveled through their journey of grief, they would need to talk to people who loved and cared for them about how they were feeling. Both Michael and Jessica began to cry. She held them and they felt her love for them.

MICHAEL suddenly became very angry and began to stamp his feet and pound the ground with his fists. "It isn't fair!" he cried. "Why did this happen? I want my mother!" Just then, a huge volcano erupted. Mrs. Beens said, "It's okay to feel angry when someone dies. That is the Volcano of Anger we are passing now."

"You told me that I would get to a place where I would feel better. When are we going to get there?" asked. Michael. "You'll see. We are now entering the Rocks of Guilt," said Mrs. Beens.

"Mother must have died because of something that
I did," Jessica said. "Sometimes I didn't listen to her,
and sometimes I was really angry at her." Michael
worried that he had done something wrong, too. "Now
children," said Mrs. Beens, "Your mother got very sick
and that was not your fault." She hugged them both
and told them that they must keep going.

M RS. Beens took their hands as they entered the Dark Woods of Fear. "I'm scared," said Michael. "Me, too," said Jessica. "What will we ever do without our mother?" the children wondered. They did not want to think about what life would be like without her. It really frightened them. "Just hold my hand," said Mrs. Beens. "You will be alright. I can tell that you are getting stronger and stronger as we travel together."

NEXT, they came to the Long Desert of Grief. "I don't want to go into the desert!" cried Jessica. "But this is part of the journey," said Mrs. Beens. "Michael and I will be right by your side as you go. I know that this is hard for you, but we must cross the desert to get to the place where you will feel better."

AFTER traveling through the Long Desert of Grief, they came to the Hills of Change. Some of the hills were big and some were small. "The hills are telling you that you will have some big changes in your life and some small changes. I know that you will be able to handle this. You are getting stronger and stronger as we travel together," said Mrs. Beens. "We are getting closer now."

SOON they came to some palm trees beside a clear blue pool. Other children were there swimming and playing. "This is the place I told you about," explained Mrs. Beens. "You will get used to life without your mother. You will still miss her very much though, and you will never forget about her. You will have happy times again. It is what your mother wanted for you."

Michael and Jessica ran to play with the other children . . .
and even laughed together.

After playing awhile, the children came and sat next to Mrs. Beens. Jessica smiled as she opened the locket and looked at her dear mother's picture. Michael took the golden watch out of his pocket. "You have helped us through a very hard time, Mrs. Beens," he said, "Thank you so much." Mrs. Beens hugged the children and smiled. "It is time for me to go and help other children. You may journey back into the Land of Grief sometimes," she explained, "but you will be alright now. Go and hug your father. He will be happy to see you. He misses your mother, too. Never forget, you are still a family."

JESSICA and Michael held hands and returned home to their castle. They felt better and knew that they would be alright. Their father helped them to put a picture of their dear mother up in their room. They all spoke of her often with great love, and they remembered all of the wonderful times they had together. They knew that their mother would always be in their hearts.

Important Information on the Grieving Preschool-Age Child

• Grieving preschoolers often have feelings of fear and confusion. They need to know that people who love them will be taking care of them. Repeating this will help the child to have feelings of security and love. They need to know someone will fix their lunch and fix their broken bike.

• Daily routine provides a "security blanket" for young children and reassures them that they are safe, secure and will continue to be cared for by people who love them. It is important to provide regular play opportunities, meal times, bath times, and "good night" routines.

• Remain as consistent as possible with behavior expectations. The grieving preschooler should be expected to obey familiar family and community rules. Consistent and appropriate discipline helps little ones maintain the safe boundaries they need.

Explaining the Death:

• Children need clear and concise information about the death, the causes and the circumstances. Provide just enough information to answer their simple questions. They may repeat the questions often; respond with the same simple answers to bolster understanding and acceptance of the death.

• It is important for a young child to gain an understanding of the permanence of death. Young children often believe the death is a fantasy and that the person will return. With young children, it is helpful to say, "He has died and is not going to eat anymore; sleep anymore, etc."

• Provide a true, simple, and brief explanation on how the person died. Use words that the young child can easily understand. One might say, "She was very sick and the doctor could not make her better." Or, "a car hit her." If the death was a suicide, the child needs to be told the truth in a brief, simple sentence, for example, "She hurt herself in a dangerous way and she died" or "He hurt himself with a gun and he died." A professional counselor will provide just the right help and words with tragic death explanations of this type or others.

Understanding the Grieving Child:

• Young children's grief reactions are expressed through their daily activities and emotional reactions. Their grief reactions are often unpredictable and spontaneous; and may occur briefly throughout the day. Very young children are not able to think about their loss for very long due to their brief attention span and their limited ability to comprehend loss.

• Much of the preschool child's behavior is refusal based. Accept the fact that "No" might become their favorite word amidst the confusion from the death and their overwhelming feelings of grief.

• Give the child permission to grieve by validating that they are feeling mad, sad, angry or scared because they are missing their person who died. They need to be reassured that these feelings are normal. Be sure to allow yourself to grieve freely in front of the child and assure them that tears are a way to get better from all the sadness.

Providing Support and Healing Play:

• Familiar times of rocking and cuddling bring a sense of security and might be just what is needed during those tearful times of grief eruptions.

• Encourage and allow the child to express their grief through creative play, art and emotions. This is how they grieve.

• Healing play ideas: 1) A special space or a homemade "tent" designated as their safe place in which to be with and/or play with their favorite toys and familiar objects until life feels better; 2) Creative play material such as Play doh, crayons and paper, finger paints, sand trays, toy figurines (people and action figures), toy houses, dolls, and puppets (easily made out of small paper bags or purchased from a toy store), and/or 3) Age-appropriate story books with themes of loss, healing and returning to feeling safe and happy.

Dedications and acknowledgements

George and Joyce Murchison, The Bess J. Hodges Foundation, and the Clancy Foundation have generously contributed to this project. We dedicate this book to their daughter Kellee Murchison Bennett.

It started like any other day for Kellee Murchison Bennett. She got up in the morning, went to work, and had lunch with her friends. Hours later, she collapsed. Despite an emergency response team's best efforts, her heart failed, and Kellee died. Kellee didn't fit the profile of a typical heart patient; she was an athletic 35 year-old wife and mother of two young boys, Tyler and Tanner. So, how does a seemingly healthy woman have a heart disease and not even know it?

Kellee's parents, George and Joyce Murchison, and her brother Michael, wanted to find a way to help other women while honoring the memory of their daughter and sister. They decided to get involved by supporting programs to provide early detection and treatment of heart disease in women at each of the three major hospitals in Long Beach, CA. The objective of the screening program is to help women identify their individual vascular disease risk factors and develop an effective strategy to modify their risk. While the grief of losing Kellee is still with the Murchisons today, they march forward in her memory with these hospital programs. The family gratefully thanks all those individuals who have helped them in this endeavor, especially New Hope Grief Support Community for remembering Kellee's legacy.

Miller Foundation has been a strong supporter of New Hope Grief Support Community and its programs. They have awarded funding for our camps and for this book, simply because of the common-hearted vision of "people helping people." We embrace their mission and focus: "Health is a state of complete and social well-being and not merely the absence of disease or infirmity." As a group with arms that extend around many causes in our community, The Miller Foundation has joined New Hope in believing that every person who grieves is important. Out of this belief, they have generously helped fund this book. Thank you, Miller Foundation!

New Hope Grief Support Community also would like to thank our OCAHU-Women in Business support team for their tenaciously dilligent fundraising efforts to provide additional funding for this book project.

A special thanks to Jillian Faith Painter, who created the name for the character Mrs. Beens. Jillian is the youngest of three children. Her family includes her brother, Jacob, and sister, Jenna, as well as parents, Gary and Patricia. Jillian's older sister Jenna passed away on December 24, 2006 when Jillian was 4 years old. As with other children who have experienced the loss of a sibling, Jenna's passing was very difficult for Jillian. After attending a grief camp conducted by New Hope Grief Support Community and going to counseling, Jillian began to learn how to live with grief. Now, she is able to help others who have experienced a similar loss.

THE TEAM OF VOLUNTEERS BEHIND Mrs. Beens:

MARSHA ANN DOBLER — AUTHOR

Marsha lives in Cypress, California with her husband Dan. She has had a long and varied career in public education. Her passion has always been to make an impact in the lives of children. New Hope Grief Support nurtured her through the loss of her mother in 1998.

Marsha's inspiration for this book was a gift from God. She dedicates this story to Him, to her sister Marilyn, and to children everywhere who have lost someone dear to them.

SUSAN K. BEENEY — STORY AND CONCEPT

Susan K. Beeney R.N. is the founder and executive director of New Hope Grief Support Community, a non-profit that helps grieving people find hope and healing. She has authored the grief handbook *A Journey of Hope* and co-authored *A Kid's Journey of Grief: Activity Handbook for Children* with Jo Anne Chung B.S.N. Susan resides in Long Beach, California with her husband, Rick who shares her passion to help those on their journey of grief find "new normal/new different".

JULIE KOCHER — ILLUSTRATION - WATERCOLORS

Julie Kocher earned a Bachelor of Fine Arts degree from Biola University in La Mirada, California, and resides in San Diego. She grew up with a love for words and pictures, and believes that one is never too old to pick up a children's book. Julie has a passion for the picture book format and its rich potential to speak meaningfully to all ages. This is her first illustrated book.
www.juliekocher.com

ALLISON OH — ILLUSTRATION - DRAWINGS

Allison Oh is a photographer, mixed-media artist and a graduate of Biola University. She is an avid fan of Japanese and American animation and enjoys cartooning and illustrating as a freelance pursuit. She merges both Eastern and Western aesthetics in her drawings and illustrations. She is currently planning to attend graduate school and pursue a career as a full-time artist.
www.allisonoh.com, allisonoh.tumblr.com

XIOMARA HARTZLER — TYPE DESIGN

Xiomara Hartzler is a freelance graphic designer, painter, illustrator and a myriad of other things. She is a native of Southern California, and received her bachelors of fine arts from Biola University. She is also interested in pursuing intercultural studies and is currently living in northern Norway.

KURT SIMONSON — ART DIRECTION

Kurt Simonson is an artist/educator who is currently a professor at Biola University. His photography projects encompass places around the globe, from a study of his childhood in Minnesota to a documentary about a family of AIDS orphans in Uganda. Kurt has previously worked with New Hope Grief Support Community the designer and photographic contributor for *A Journey of Hope*.
www.kurtsimonson.com

JOEL LUEB, BIGGERDOT — PUBLICATION

Joel is an entrepreneur and global steward involved with commercial book production. He is passionate about big ideas and connecting people to other people. He is grateful to serve as an advisory board member to New Hope Grief Support Community.
www.biggerdot.com

ABOUT NEW HOPE GRIEF SUPPORT COMMUNITY

New Hope Grief Support Community was founded by Susan K. Beeney R.N. in 1986. For the next fourteen years she provided grief support groups as a volunteer in her community. After resigning from her full time nursing position in 1999, she turned her focus on developing New Hope into a non-profit organization, which occurred in 2000. New Hope is a unique non-profit organization, offering support, care, and compassion to children and adults after the death of a loved one. The funds that are donated and raised are used for our grief support programs for children, teens and adults and our family camps. Specially trained volunteers provide education, guidance, and a safe place for people to share their experiences and emotions, without judgment or expectations. As our mission statement says, "New Hope Grief Support Community helps grieving people find hope and healing." New Hope cannot take away the grief and loss, but we can help others walk on their journey towards peace, restored life, and a "new normal."
Visit **www.newhopegrief.org** for more information.

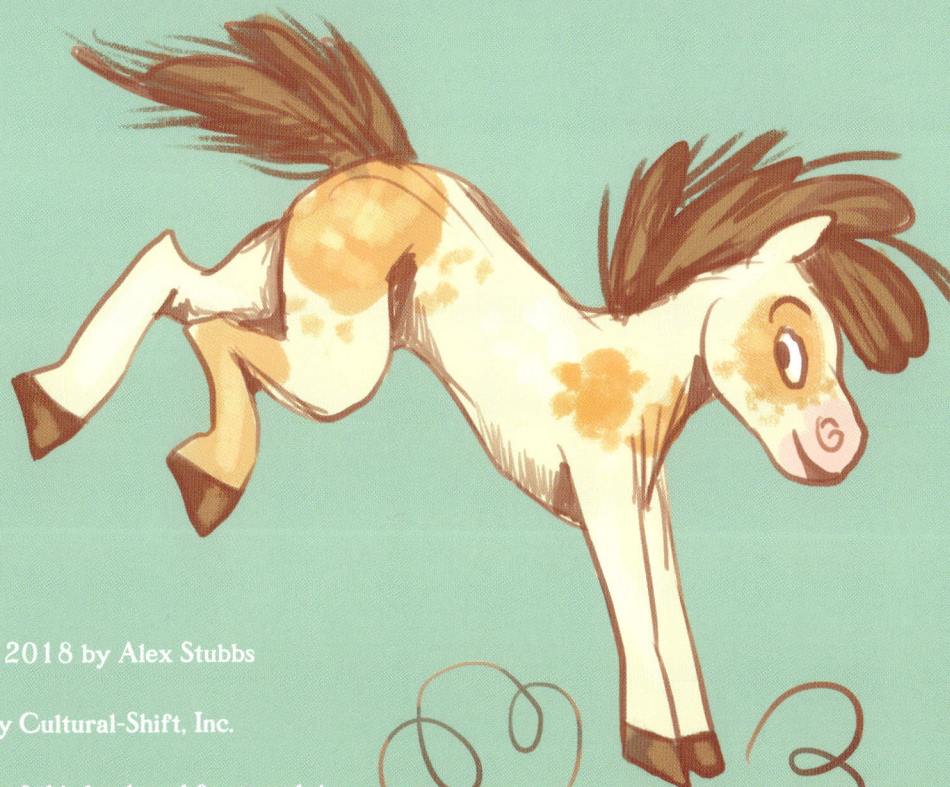

ISBN 978-1-7338750-7-3 (Hardcover) ISBN 978-1-7338750-1-1 (eBook)
Library of Congress Cataloging-in-Publication Data is available upon request.
Visit us on the Web! - www.PaperPeteBooks.com

Written, Illustrated, and Printed in Sarasota, Florida, United States of America.

First Edition Paper Pete May 2019

P.B. DISRUPTS SCHOOL!

Inspired By Hannah Stubbs

By David A. Stubbs II

Paper Pete

Illustrated By Alex Stubbs